SKY LIZARD

We shine brightest at that
which was meant for us.

Flytrap Press

www.FlytrapPress.com

JOHN EUDICONE

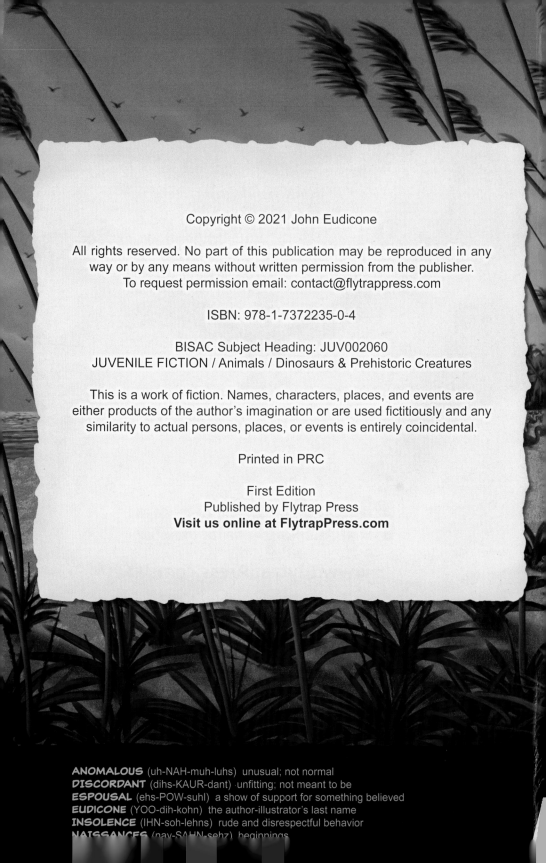

ISBN: 978-1-7372235-0-4

BISAC Subject Heading: JUV002060
JUVENILE FICTION / Animals / Dinosaurs & Prehistoric Creatures

Printed in PRC

First Edition
Published by Flytrap Press
Visit us online at FlytrapPress.com

ANOMALOUS (uh-NAH-muh-luhs) unusual; not normal
DISCORDANT (dihs-KAUR-dant) unfitting; not meant to be
ESPOUSAL (ehs-POW-suhl) a show of support for something believed
EUDICONE (YOO-dih-kohn) the author-illustrator's last name
INSOLENCE (IHN-soh-lehns) rude and disrespectful behavior
NAISSANCES (nay-SAHN-sehz) beginnings

Contents

PROVENANCE (PRAH-veh-nans) where something is originally from
PROVIDENCE (PRAH-vih-dehns) future security
QUA (KWAH) serving as
RAPTORIAL (raap-TAU-ree-uhl) of birds [or reptiles] of prey
RHAPSODY (RAAP-suh-dee) the enthusiastic expression of passion
TURBULENT (TER-byoo-lehnt) of violent movement

BOWED (BOHWD) bent over
BUSTLE (BUH-sihl) energetic activity
EMERGED (eh-MERJD) came out from
INTENT (ihn-TEHNT) with purpose
PALLID (PAA-lihd) faded in color; pale
QUIVERING (KWIH-ver-ing) shaking slightly

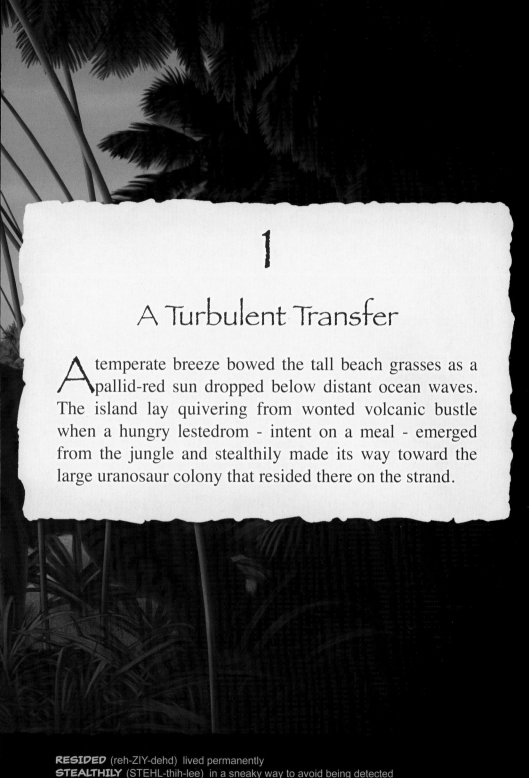

1

A Turbulent Transfer

A temperate breeze bowed the tall beach grasses as a pallid-red sun dropped below distant ocean waves. The island lay quivering from wonted volcanic bustle when a hungry lestedrom - intent on a meal - emerged from the jungle and stealthily made its way toward the large uranosaur colony that resided there on the strand.

RESIDED (reh-ZIY-dehd) lived permanently
STEALTHILY (STEHL-thih-lee) in a sneaky way to avoid being detected
STRAND (STRAND) the shore of a body of water; beach
TEMPERATE (TEHM-per-eht) mild in temperature
VOLCANIC (vaul-KAN-ihk) of a volcano
WONTED (WAHN-tehd) what is normal and expected; the usual

ADOPTED (uh-DAHP-tehd) took on; assumed
ALTERED (AUL-terd) changed
OPPORTUNITY (ah-paur-TOO-nih-tee) chance to get what is wanted
PACE (PAYS) speed of travel

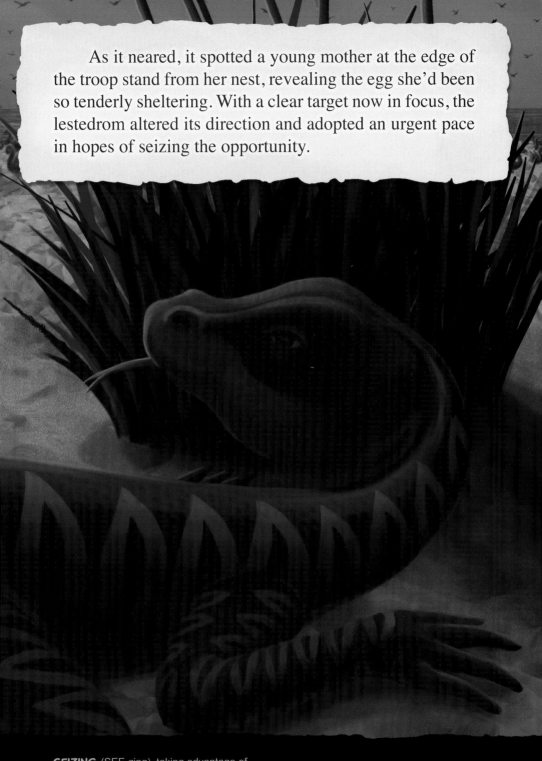

As it neared, it spotted a young mother at the edge of the troop stand from her nest, revealing the egg she'd been so tenderly sheltering. With a clear target now in focus, the lestedrom altered its direction and adopted an urgent pace in hopes of seizing the opportunity.

SEIZING (SEE-zing) taking advantage of
SHELTERING (SHEHL-ter-ing) protecting
TENDERLY (TEHN-der-lee) with love and gentleness
TROOP (TROOP) large group of the same kind of animal

…Now within range - and still undetected - it opened its mouth and snatched its prize while the mother was tending to her distraction, but it wasn't long before the mother caught wind of an unfamiliar scent and looked back to see about its source.

"Oh no!" She shrieked, upon realizing the spot where her egg once rested was empty.

She looked up in a panic and scanned the beach with desperate eyes for an explanation - where she noticed the lestedrom, dashing away…*with her egg*! With an adrenaline-fueled fury, she thrust open her wings and took to the air in a fervent quest to reclaim her treasure. Amidst her flight, she imparted an onslaught of harrowing hollers and accompanying cries that did nothing to slow the thief as it sprinted back toward the jungle.

Her rapid ascent up the sand was commendable but despite her best effort the lestedrom reached its refuge and slipped into the foliage. Undaunted, the mother kept flapping and sailed in after it - delivered by tunnel vision to a place a tranquil mind would never venture.

AMIDST (uh-MIHDST) during
ASCENT (uh-SEHNT) upward travel
COMMENDABLE (kuh-MEHN-duh-buhl) praiseworthy
FERVENT (FER-vehnt) highly emotional
FOLIAGE (FOH-lee-ehj) plant leaves
HARROWING (HAA-roh-wing) terrifying

ONSLAUGHT (AHN-slaut) overwhelming amount
QUEST (KWEHST) serious attempt to get something important
REFUGE (REH-fyooj) place of protection; shelter
TRANQUIL (TRAYN-kwihl) calm
TUNNEL VISION complete focus on one thing
UNDAUNTED (uhn-DAUN-tehd) not discouraged
VENTURE (VEHN-cher) risk visiting because of the danger involved

The jungle interior was noticeably darker and dense vegetation with dangling vines made flying impossible, so she dropped to the ground and continued her chase on foot. In here, with apposite markings, the lestedrom was barely visible - its course mostly evident by the clattering undergrowth it scurried through.

APPOSITE (AA-puh-siht) very fitting; appropriate
ARRAY (uh-RAY) wide variety
COURSE (KAURS) direction of travel
ENDURED (ehn-DERD) suffered through
EVIDENT (EH-vih-dehnt) clearly visible
IMPETUS (IHM-peh-tuhs) motivation
OBLIVIOUS (ah-BLIH-vee-uhs) completely unaware

They slalomed in tandem at a demanding pace, amid an array of overgrown shin-tangle, but the occasional glimpse of her egg traversing the leaves offered the impetus the mother needed to persist. Oblivious to the pain of penetrating thorns and a pulmonary itch from inhaled gnats, she endured the ordeal as the remaining light dwindled to darkness.

ORDEAL (aur-DEE-uhl) unpleasant experience
PENETRATING (PEH-neh-tray-ting) piercing
PULMONARY (PUHL-muh-naa-ree) of the lungs
SHIN-TANGLE (SHIHN-tayn-guhl) small bushes and plantlife
SLALOMED (SLAH-luhmd) ran in a zigzag pattern
TANDEM (TAN-dehm) one right behind the other
TRAVERSING (truh-VER-sing) traveling throu..

The cadence continued to a miry peatland, of sorts, with ferns full of flickering fireflies and a chorus of resident peepers. Here, the mother found herself struggling to keep up - beset by the slippery, moss laden branches strewn about the area.

BEHEMOTH (beh-HEE-muhth) something that is very large
BESET (beh-SEHT) held back; troubled
CADENCE (KAY-dehns) speed of travel
CHORUS (KAU-ruhs) singing group
GIRTH (GERTH) measurment around the middle

The lestedrom, however, was clearly at home and soon began to outdistance her. It made its way to a well-worn path that led to a log of staggering girth and vanished inside the hollowed-out end of the behemoth.

MIRY (MIY-ree) wet and muddy
PEATLAND (PEET-land) swamp
PEEPERS (PEE-perz) little frogs
RESIDENT (REH-zih-dehnt) long-term dwelling
STAGGERING (STAA-ger-ing) very surprising
STREWN (STROOWN) scattered

13

Upon reaching the path, the mother was spent. Her torso shook from the pounding behind her breastbone as she wobbled on weary legs toward the opening of the log. She staggered to the edge of its dry-rotted bark and peered past the mushrooms into the gloom, hoping for a sign of her egg, but all she could detect was a rhythmic wheeze at the far end of the blackness. Despite trepidation, she cut short her respite and skulked toward the sound - bracing for the unexpected.

BREASTBONE (BREHST-bohn) bone at the center of the chest that covers the heart
DESPITE (dehs-PIYT) in spite of
PEERED (PEARD) looked with a fixed focus
RHYTHMIC (RIHTHUH-mihk) repeated with regular timing
RESPITE (REHS-piht) rest period

SKULKED (SKUHLKT) walked in a cautious manner
SPENT (SPEHNT) very tired
TORSO (TAUR-soh) trunk of the body
TREPIDATION (treh-pih-DAY-shuhn) fear of what might happen
WHEEZE (WEEZ) raspy breathing

ENSUING (ehn-SOO-ing) following
LIGNEOUS (LIHG-nee-uhs) made of wood particles

Each step on the damp interior wood caused it to splinter and cake underfoot. The ligneous buildup continued as she plodded further inside. As she drew near, the noise suddenly stopped – leaving her scales to crawl in the ensuing silence - then, without warning, the lestedrom lunged.

LUNGED (LUHNJD) suddenly thrust forward
PLODDED (PLAH-dehd) walked with slow, heavy steps

17

The impact knocked her aside, but as it slipped past she reached out with her talons and latched onto its tail - halting its escape. The lestedrom turned and hissed incessantly while writhing to free itself from her grasp but the mother held on steadfastly. She pulled on the appendage

APPENDAGE (uh-PEHN-dehj) body part
ELUSIVE (eh-LOO-sihv) difficult to catch
HINDERED (HIHN-derd) made difficult
IMPACT (IHM-paakt) force of collision
INCESSANTLY (ihn-SEH-sehnt) without interruption; nonstop

with all she had, but her grip - hindered by the coating of previously acquired particles - began slipping and the elusive creature soon wriggled itself loose and scrambled away. With a well-timed second wind the mother went after it - out of the log and across the path, where the chase resumed in the tenebrous verdure.

STEADFASTLY (STEHD-faast-lee) without giving up
TALONS (TAA-luhnz) claws [that are found on raptor toes]
TENEBROUS (TEH-neh-bruhs) dark and shadowy
VERDURE (VER-jyer) lush, green plant life
WRITHING (RIY-thing) twisting and struggling

After a lengthy stretch of arduous scuffling the landscape began to change; heavily wooded conditions gave way to an increasingly rocky terrain. The dwindling tree count and scant flora offered the mother a chance to fly again, so with outspread wings she launched herself upward and began flapping under the sparse canopy. Now in her element, she rocketed toward the lestedrom as it loped over vestiges of bygone slayings on the moonlit jungle floor.

SCANT (SKANT) small in amount
SCUFFLING (SKUH-fuh-ling) awkward, hurried travel
SLAYINGS (SLAY-ingz) killings of animals
SPARSE (SPAHRS) in small, scattered amounts
TERRAIN (teh-RAYN) land
VESTIGES (VEHS-tih-jehz) small pieces

She caught up to the creature near a cluster of sarsens and began her descent with outstretched talons. The diminishing distance between them bode promise and she soon had it within reach, but just as the tips of her talons made contact the jaws of a cryptognat sprang from the stones and ripped the lestedrom from her clutch. She slammed to the ground from the force of the clash and watched helplessly as a second appeared with a deep vocal eruption and tried to steal the catch from the first. The first quickly swung its head to avoid it - causing the lestedrom to release the egg - but before the mother could get to her feet the second had turned its attention to her.

ERUPTION (eh-RUHP-shuhn) sudden outbreak
PROMISE (PRAH-mihs) cause to expect that what is wanted will happen
SARSENS (SAHR-sehnz) boulders
VOCAL (VOH-kuhl) of the voice

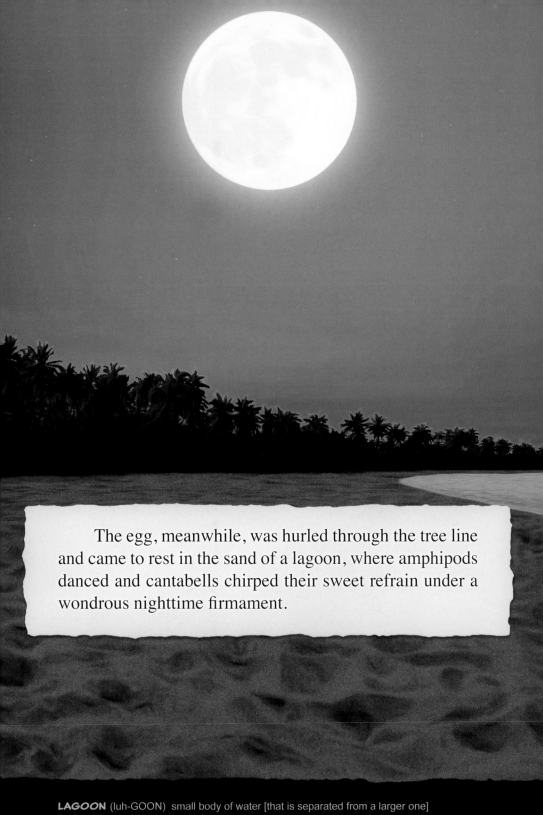

The egg, meanwhile, was hurled through the tree line and came to rest in the sand of a lagoon, where amphipods danced and cantabells chirped their sweet refrain under a wondrous nighttime firmament.

LAGOON (luh-GOON) small body of water [that is separated from a larger one]
REFRAIN (ree-FRAYN) repeating sound
WONDROUS (WUHN-druhs) beautiful and interesting

2

Anomalous Naissances

The next afternoon found the battered eggshell critically heated under a blistering mid-day sun, prompting the blood-stained hatchling within it to escape from its oven. It twisted and squirmed until the leathery enclosure was breached and an expanding tear allowed for its release into existence.

It opened its eyes and blinked to clear the dried spatter from a gash on its brow as the image of a large bellusala, fanning its wings on a nearby rock, slowly came into focus. The motion and brilliant azure coloring of the insect beckoned the hatchling's examination, so it struggled to its feet and went in for a closer look.

BREACHED (BREECHT) broke through
CRITICALLY (KRIH-tih-kuh-lee) to a high degree
ENCLOSURE (ehn-KLOH-zhər) surrounding barrier

27

After a long inquisitive gaze, a gentle nudge from its snout sent the creature fluttering down the beach. The hatchling toddled after it, with an occasional fall in the sand, until it could no longer keep up and just sat in the silt near the edge of the water.

A short time later, a brawny male thallasaur came sauntering up the shoreline - overturning rocks as he went. He held a finful of lithodon (a small, soft-shelled crustacean he enjoyed as a snack) and was searching for more when he spotted the hatchling and went to investigate.

"Well, hello little fella!" he said in a cheerful tone, as he knelt down beside it and extended a fin to pat its head. "What are you doing here all by yourself?"

The hatchling looked up in wonderment and blinked with each comforting tap it received.

"You want to go fishing? Huh?" he joked while patting. "Ha-ha, you're not ready to swim yet but maybe you're still hungry, why don't you try one of these…"

BRAWNY (BRAU-nee) strong and muscular
CRUSTACEAN (kruh-STAY-shuhn) sea creature with a shell or crust

SAUNTERING (SAUN-ter-ing) walking in a slow, relaxed manner
SILT (SIHLT) fine, sandy soil
WONDERMENT (WUHN-der-mehnt) a state of awe or great admiration

He plucked a lithodon from his fin with his mouth and dangled it above the hatchling's head as the hatchling looked up and instinctively opened its mouth so it could be dropped inside.

"Ooh, you like that," he said, as the hatchling scoffed it down. "Here, have another..."

The second went down as quickly as the first and the hatchling rejoiced in the experience.

"Well, you can't stay here," the thallasaur continued. "You'll be washed away when the tide comes in. Let's get you to higher ground."

He scooped up the hatchling in his available fin and walked it up to the top of the beach, where he set it down in the sand.

"Okay, I have to be going now. Run along and find your mother," he said with a smile as he started back in the direction from which he originally came.

The hatchling watched in silence as the thallasaur strode off and melded into the horizon - when belongingness spurred it to follow...

It jumped to its feet and scampered in the sand until he was once again visible, then tailed him back to a large thallasaur colony on the eastern shore of the island where his mate was roosting at their nest.

BELONGINGNESS (beh-LAUN-ging-nehs) the desire to belong to a group
DANGLED (DAYN-guhld) hung loosely over
HORIZON (hau-RIY-zuhn) where the earth and sky meet in the distance
INSTINCTIVELY (ihn-STINK-tihv-lee) without thinking first
MELDED (MEHL-dehd) blended together

REJOICED (ree-JOIST) showed a great feeling of joy
ROOSTING (ROOS-ting) resting
SCOFFED (SKAUFT) gobbled
SPURRED (SPERD) encouraged
STRODE (STROHD) walked

BEAMED (BEEMD) shouted with joy
BLUSTERY (BLUHS-ter-ee) very windy
GESTURED (JEHS-cherd) conveyed by motioning with his body [rather than using words]

"Yarma…" he called, as he approached her and gestured to his fin. "I brought something back for you from the lagoon."

"I see," she replied, while motioning to the hatchling as it caught up behind him. "Who's this, Zayle?"

"Oh my, he must've followed me from the lagoon. I found him there alone."

"Isn't he a cutie…what happened to his brow?"

"I don't know - but it doesn't look serious," said Zayle, to the rumble of thunder in the distance. "There's a storm coming now, but I suppose I can lead him back tomorrow."

Ominous clouds soon darkened the sky and the first squall of rain began pelting the area, so they huddled together with the hatchling between them to wait out the blustery weather.

Conditions continued the rest of the evening, and they managed to sleep through a tempestuous night, but the following morning the sky was clear when Yarma awoke to a tussle beneath her.

"Zayle…wake up!" she beamed.

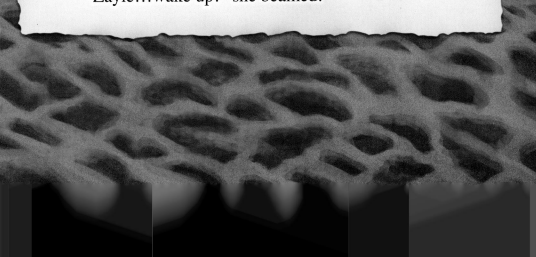

AROSE (uh-ROHZ) woke up and stood
BEHELD (bee-HEHLD) saw [something remarkable]
EXUBERANCE (ehk-ZOO-ber-ans) cheerful excitement
GAPE (GAYP) wide open mouth
GOGGLED (GAH-guhld) looked with wide open eyes

Zayle arose to her joyous inflections and gasped in exuberance at what he beheld, for there in the nest lay their newly hatched progeny. She sat up and stretched by her vacated shell, then goggled the hatchling who stood just beyond the soft grass nest lining.

The hatchling returned her curious stare and maintained his gape as she tottered over to greet him. They nuzzled for a moment at the edge of the nest, then jumped to the sand - where they romped around as the parents looked on.

"Oh, look how nicely they play together." said Yarma.

"Yeah, she really likes him," Zayle replied.

"So, we'll be calling her 'Thera'?"

"Just like we said - if it was a girl."

"…Maybe it would be good if Thera had a companion," Yarma wondered, as the hatchlings continued their frolicking. "Let's raise him with her."

"Okay," Zayle nodded, as he leaned toward the ruckus. "then he gets the boy's name… Come here Caylem, we're going to keep you around for a while."

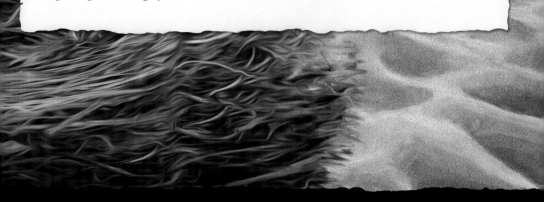

INFLECTIONS (ihn-FLEHK-shuhnz) changes in pitch of the voice
JOYOUS (JOY-uhs) full of joy
PROGENY (PRAH-jeh-nee) child
ROMPED (RAHMPT) played energetically
VACATED (VAY-kay-tehd) abandoned

FLOURISHED (F

3

The Sting of Insolence

The new family flourished over the passing months and the growing hatchlings were soon exploring the area on their own. One day, while skirting the beach grass together, they came upon a creature lying motionless in the sand.

"Wow, look at the size of that lithodon!" exclaimed Caylem, as he stooped down for a closer look. "I'm still full from the fish Daddy caught but maybe we can save it for later."

"There aren't any lithodon in this area, and why would it be out in the open like this?" Thera replied.

"I can't tell if it's even alive," said Caylem, as he poked it with a talon.

Suddenly, the creature stood up with jutted pincers and whipped its barbed tail overhead in preparation to strike.

"Caylem get back! That's a dryptocaud, and they have a nasty sting!" cried Thera.

Caylem shot backward before he could be harmed, and the two scarpered for safety as the creature slinked into the grasses.

"…You almost got stung back there," huffed Thera, as their scuttling slowed some distance away. "Let's stay near the water for a while."

AMBLED (AM-buhld) walked at a relaxed pace
BEVY (BEH-vee) large group
DETRITUS (deh-TRIY-tuhs) loose debris and waste
EBBING (EH-bing) moving away from shore
IRIDESCENT (EA-rih-deh-sehnt) having colors that change when moved

A shaken Caylem agreed, so they ambled along the ebbing tidewater, amidst fellow thallasaur bevy members and washed up detritus, when Thera stopped to admire the scintillating seashells embedded in the wet sand.

"Oh, cool..." she said, as she crouched to inspect one's iridescent nacre.

She collected a number of shells in her fin and walked them up to dryer ground, where she sat and laid them out for comparison.

"What do you plan on doing with those?" asked Caylem, as he surveyed the arrangement.

"...Let's see who can make the taller tower," Thera suggested, as she began stacking them with her mouth.

Caylem accepted her challenge and went to gather a pile of his own. Upon returning, he dumped his collection in the sand next to hers and set to work. Using one foot to perch on and the other to stack, he placed each shell with considerable care, and before long, the height of his stack had surpassed Thera's considerably.

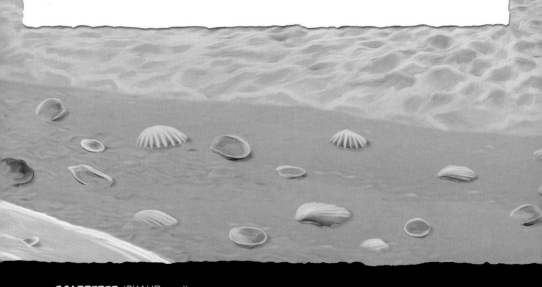

SCARPERED (SKAHR-perd) ran away
SCINTILLATING (SIHN-tih-lay-ting) sparkling while shining brightly
SCUTTLING (SKUH-tuh-ling) quick paced walking
SLINKED (SLINKT) left quietly
NACRE (NAY-ker) inside lining

41

"Wow, your tower's looking good!" exclaimed Thera, as she stood from the sand and brushed herself off. "I'm going to get more shells for mine..."

EXCLAIMED (ehk

ABSENCE (AAB-sehns) not being there
EVALUATE (eh-VAAL-yoo-ayt) judge
HANDIWORK (HAN-dee-werk) handmade creation

Caylem continued working in her absence, and his handiwork caught the attention of two older thallasaur juveniles who happened by.

"What're ya makin' there?" called Olly (the larger of the two), as they approached.

"I'm playing a game with my sister to see who can make the taller tower," Caylem smiled back proudly, as he stopped to evaluate his progress. "...It's almost as tall as I am now!"

"Yeah, well why're ya doin' it with y'ur *foot*?" Olly reproached.

"That's just how I do it," Caylem shrugged.

"Look out, I'll show ya the *right* way ta do it..." Olly snapped, as he reached for a shell with his teeth.

JUVENILES (JOO-vih-nuhlz) youths
REPROACHED (ree-PROHCHT) responded with disapproval
SNAPPED (SNAAPT) said with irritation

45

Caylem looked on as Olly loomed over the stack with a shell in his mouth, pondering how best to place it, but when he tried to set it down the stack toppled over.

"...Looks like ya lost the game," he blurted, with a mound of fallen shells at his feet.

Caylem stood in reticent dismay while Olly and his pal guffawed over the incident.

BLURTED (BLER-tehd) said without thinking first
CONSTERNATION (KAHN-ster-nay-shuhn) stress
DISMAY (dihs-MAY) sudden disappointment
GUFFAWED (guh-FAUD) laughed loudly

"…I got 'n idea for a better game," he continued, as their laughter died down. "Let's see who can throw 'em the furthest in the water!"

Caylem watched with increased consternation as they kicked over Thera's tower and began flinging shells into the water.

INCIDENT (IHN-sih-dehnt) happening; event
LOOMED (LOOMD) stood over in a threatening way
PONDERING (PAHN-der-ing) thinking about
RETICENT (REH-tih-sehnt) without showing thoughts or feelings

"…What happened to our towers?" sighed Thera, as she returned to their mirth with a new pile of shells.

"These guys knocked them down," an expressionless Caylem grumbled, as the bullies continued their horseplay.

CONCURRED (ku
MILIEU (mihl-YOC

"...Come on, let's go," Thera frowned, after dropping her pile and starting away. Caylem concurred, and they left the milieu for less vacuous surroundings.

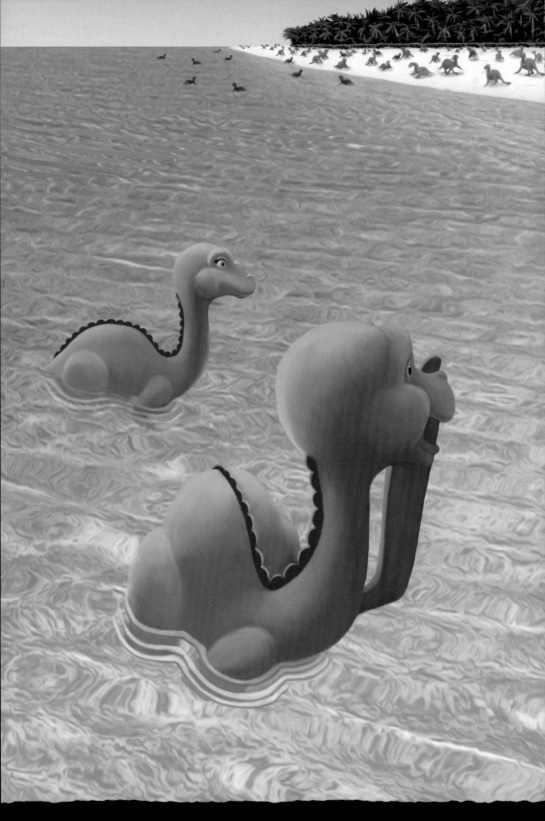

SIBLINGS (SIHB-lingz) children of the same parents [brother and sister]

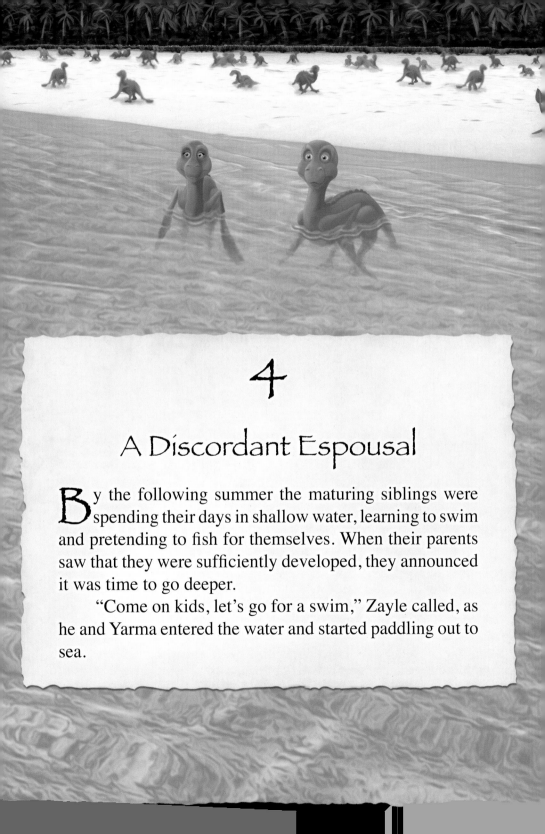

4

A Discordant Espousal

By the following summer the maturing siblings were spending their days in shallow water, learning to swim and pretending to fish for themselves. When their parents saw that they were sufficiently developed, they announced it was time to go deeper.

"Come on kids, let's go for a swim," Zayle called, as he and Yarma entered the water and started paddling out to sea.

Thera eagerly followed - piercing the oncoming surfs with little effort - but when Caylem attempted the same he discovered he wasn't as buoyant. His flapping and kicking did little to keep him afloat, so he helped with his feet by pushing off the shoal - until the water got too deep to continue, then all he could do was splash in place with

his head bobbing in and out of the water while his family forged ahead.

"Wait for me!" he gasped, as ocean spray invaded his nostrils and tingled his turbinal lining.

He started to sneeze and began to turn back when something bumped into the side of his head.

COMBERS (KOH-merz) long, curling waves
CONVENED (kahn-VEEND) got together to talk
GAWP (GAUP) rude stare
MIEN (MEEN) way of doing something [that expresses how one feels about doing it]
OMINOUS (AH-mih-nuhs) threatening

He looked and saw that it was a piece of driftwood that had been carried over by the waves. As it floated past he reached out with his wings and pulled himself onto it - finding it kept him afloat nicely, then sculled after his family with it positioned under his chest.

"Attaboy Caylem, you're doing great son!" Zayle encouraged, as Caylem brought up the rear.

The family enjoyed a pleasant afternoon of swimming together and when they returned to the beach Caylem saved the driftwood for subsequent use. He practiced with it each day, and before long he was treading water as well as Thera.

One day, while swimming alongshore with her, she surged ahead and proposed a challenge: "You've been getting faster lately, but I bet you still can't catch me!"

"We'll see..." Caylem replied, as he lowered his head and poured on his power.

They raced through the swells with a spirited mien, trying hard to outdo one another, but when Caylem passed Olly in neighboring combers his strokes became more about fleeing than vying. The bully peered over as Caylem swam past and summoned his buddy, who waded nearby, and the two convened with an ominous vibe as Caylem sought to escape their gawp.

SUBSEQUENT (SUHB-seh-kwehnt) happening later in time; future
SUMMONED (SUH-muhnd) called urgently
SWELLS (SWEHLZ) rising ocean waves
TREADING (TREH-ding) traveling through
VIBE (VIYB) expression of emotion
VYING (VIY-ing) competing

A short distance later, when feeling more safe, Caylem glanced back to allay his concerns but incurred new presentiment at the sight of them following. He continued askance with the duo in tow until they finally caught up and flanked him.

"…Ha-ha, lookit them goofy flippers!" Olly jeered, as he watched Caylem's paddling.

Caylem tried to ignore him, but things got more tense when he latched onto the driftwood and made a demand:

ALLAY (uh-LAY) calm
ASKANCE (uh-SKANS) with suspicion and mistrust
CONCERNS (kuhn-SERNZ) fears
DUO (DOO-oh) team of two
FLANKED (FLAYNKT) got on both sides of
IGNORE (ihg-NAWR) pay no attention to

"Hey, lemme try the wood."

"There's plenty of wood around here for you to try if you want," said Thera, after dropping back to intervene.

"No one's talkin' ta you!" Olly snapped, before swiping his fin to splash her.

"You gotta learn ta share." he continued, as he turned to Caylem and began wrenching the wood out from under him.

Caylem resisted but it was no use, the bully was stronger and soon overpowered him. He slid off the wood and thrashed about as the water engulfed him. Thera went to help, but before she could reach him his frantic movements turned methodical and he found himself swimming to shore unaided. Upon reaching shallow water, he stood up and panted as the water drained from his wings and wonderment flooded his thoughts.

"Caylem, you swam on your own! You don't need the wood anymore!" Thera cried, as she came up behind him.

Grasping her verity, and its importance to fishing for himself, he turned to her and made an avowal: "I'm going to work hard and be the best swimmer I can be!"

"I know you will," Thera smiled, as she waded toward the beach to exit the water. "…Let's head home now."

"Let's *swim* back," replied Caylem, with an extended wing to halt her.

AVOWAL (uh-VOW-uhl) declaration of intent; promise
ENGULFED (ehn-GUHLFT) swallowed completely
HALT (HAULT) stop
FRANTIC (FRAN-tihk) wild and uncontrolled
METHODICAL (meh-THAH-dih-kuhl) orderly and controlled

PANTED (PAN-tehd) breathed heavily
RESISTED (reh-ZIHS-tehd) fought back
THRASHED (THRAASHT) whacked violently
UNAIDED (uhn-AY-dehd) without help
VERITY (VEA-rih-tee) truth

ALLURE (uh-LER) ability to attract and fascinate
ASSENTED (uh-SEHN-tehd) agreed
BENTHIC (BEHN-thihk) of the ocean floor
BIOME (BIY-ohm) community of plants and animals
CONSISTENT (kuhn-SIHS-tehnt) regular
ENHANCE (ehn-HANS) make even better

5

Surprise Catch

After several months of consistent practice, Caylem's swimming had advanced to the point where he was diving with Thera to view the marvelous biome that graced the ocean floor. Giant clams bearing lustrous pearls and colorful nudibranch were among the inhabitants to enhance its allure.

Zayle took notice of their benthic excursions and suggested to Yarma that the youngsters were ready to try some fishing.

"Let's head to the saltmarsh with the kids tomorrow," he said. "The fish there are slower and will be easier for them to catch."

Yarma assented, and they left the next morning to follow the plan.

EXCURSIONS (eks-KER-zhuhnz) short trips
INHABITANTS (ihn-HAA-bih-tants) things that lived there
LUSTROUS (LUHS-truhs) shiny
MARVELOUS (MAHR-veh-luhs) wonderful
NUDIBRANCH (NOO-dih-braynk) sea slugs
SALTMARSH (SAULT-mahrsh) salt water wetland

When the family arrived at the picturesque mere it was teeming with saltoneus. The lissome fish glistened in the sunlight as they popped from the water to snatch dragonflies from overhead airstreams.

"Alright kids, wait here while we circle around and herd some fish toward you," Zayle instructed, after they entered the water.

The youngsters complied and sparkled with merriment as their parents swam off.

Within a short time, the parents had a small school rounded up and were driving them back toward the ambuscade.

"Here they come!" Caylem shouted, before plunging to intercept them.

He wafted with Thera through a barrage of fish, nipping with zeal until the last had passed, but surfaced with nothing to show for it. Thera, meanwhile, wallowed beside him, exulting over her first capture.

AMBUSCADE (AM-buhs-kayd) attackers [waiting to attack by surprise]
BARRAGE (buh-RAHZH) very large number
COMPLIED (kuhm-PLIYD) did as told
EXULTING (ehks-UHL-ting) loudly celebrating
HERD (HERD) direct the direction of travel of
INTERCEPT (ihn-ter-SEHPT) seize something before it gets to where it is going

MERE (MEAR) body of water
MERRIMENT (MEH-rih-mehnt) the joy of having fun
PICTURESQUE (pihk-cher-EHSK) beautiful enough to photograph
TEEMING (TEE-ming) full of
WAFTED (WAHF-tehd) passed through easily
WALLOWED (WAH-lohwd) took great pleasure in
ZEAL (ZEE-uhl) great desire

"Way to go, Thera!" Zayle extolled, as she tipped back her head and gobbled it down. "...Let's try again so Caylem can get one."

The family retried - until late afternoon, reprising the scene with unvarying results until Thera was sated and could not continue.

"Okay kids, that's enough for today," said Zayle, as he and Yarma exited the water. "Let's head home now."

Caylem glanced down with a somber countenance and let out a sigh, when Thera came up to assuage him. "Don't feel bad," she said. "We'll come back tomorrow, and you'll catch one then."

The following day they returned on their own to see if he'd fare any better. After entering the water, Thera swam off to round up some fish but found them too intractable.

"Ugh...I can't herd these fish by myself!" she bellowed in frustration.

Just then, Caylem heard footfall nearby. He looked and saw Olly perambulating with his pal at the edge of the water.

"Maybe we should just go," he blurted in angst.

"No, wait...I have an idea..." replied Thera.

She snapped the culm of a reed with her teeth and proffered its inflorescence.

"Try waving this over the water," she said. "You might fool a fish into jumping out at you."

ANGST (AYN-gst) a feeling of dread
ASSUAGE (uh-SWAYJ) help feel better
BELLOWED (BEH-lohwd) complained loudly
COUNTENANCE (KAHN-teh-nehns) look on his face
CULM (KUHLM) stem
EXTOLLED (ehks-TOHLD) praised highly
FRUSTRATION (fruh-STRAY-shuhn) emotional irritation from repeated failure

INFLORESCENCE (ihn-flaur-EH-sehns) flowering end
INTRACTABLE (ihn-TRAAK-tuh-buhl) hard to control
PERAMBULATING (per-AM-byoo-lay-ting) walking without a destination
PROFFERED (PRAH-ferd) held out for acceptance
REPRISING (reh-PRIY-zing) doing again
SATED (SAY-tehd) fully satisfied
SOMBER (SAHM-ber) sad

Caylem was skeptical but agreed to try. He took the end of the stalk in his mouth and began waving as directed.

"Ha-ha, what's he supposta be doin'?" mocked Olly. "Now he looks like even more of a dork then usual."

"Just ignore him," said Thera, while backing away. "This time you'll nail 'em Caylem!" she cheered with conviction.

ACCELERATED (aak-SEHL-er-ay-tehd) suddenly swam faster
BEGUILED (beh-GIY-uhld) fooled into wanting
BRIMMED (BRIHMD) overflowed
CLUSTERED (KLUHS-terd) gathered together
CONVICTION (kuhn-VIHK-shuhn) certainty
MAW (MAU) mouth

Before long, several fish came stalking. The beguiled group clustered a few feet from the reed as it wigwagged over the water. Caylem brimmed with excitement over the prospect of catching one and poised himself in preparation, when one broke from the pack and accelerated toward him. As it popped from the water he readied to seize it with widened eyes and a ravenous maw, but the fish missed the reed and clamped on his snout.

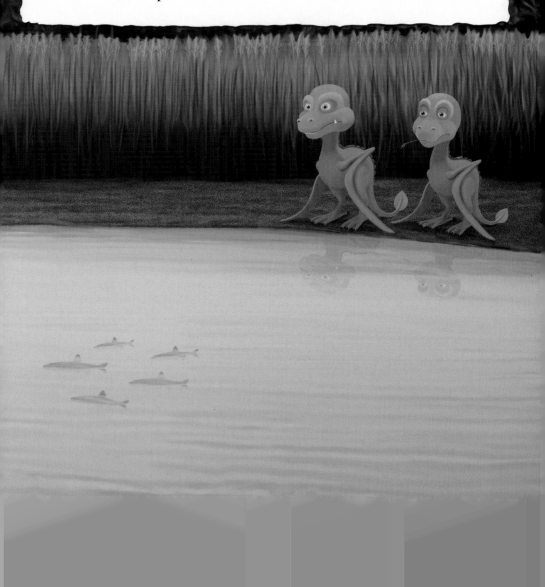

CHAGRIN (shuh-(
CHORTLED (CHA

It clung to the tip with a discomfiting waggle until Caylem's swift wing smote it back to the water.

"Ha-ha! *'Nail* 'em Caylem?' You mean *'Fail* 'em Caylem!'" Olly scoffed. "The fish caught *him*!"

Caylem turned to hide his chagrin and proceeded to exit the water as the bullies chortled behind him.

"Where are you going? You almost had it!" cried Thera. "Try again!"

"No, I'm tired of fishing," Caylem replied, in a dissimulative tone. "Let's go to the lagoon for some lithodon."

Thera was sure he'd catch one but just shook her head and went to join him.

6

Flight-by-Flight

By the equinoctial tide's return Thera had vanquished the trials of nonage. Fully fledged and out on her own, she fished ably in the vernal waters. Caylem, however, was not as accomplished. Although mature, he had yet to experience his first capture.

One morning, after another fruitless attempt, he broached to find Olly drawing a shot of seaweed stipe athwart his path to shore. The vegetal line stretched to his buddy, who anchored the opposite end. Bemused, Caylem tarried as the snickering bully encircled him.

When the line had looped his sensitive midriff, Olly widened his grin and yanked it taut – rousing the jellyfish he'd knotted in the fronds.

NONAGE (NOH-nehj) youth
ROUSING (ROW-zing) stimulating activity; exciting
SHOT (SHAHT) nautical measurment equal to 90 feet
TARRIED (TAA-reed) stayed longer than necessary
VANQUISHED (VAYN-kwihsht) overcome
VEGETAL (VEH-jih-tuhl) of plantlife

Caylem yowled and fought to free himself as a throng of gelatinous tentacles seared his integument.

The fray continued until Thera arrived in response to his cries and helped unfetter him.

"What happened?" she asked, as the bullies departed.

"That jerk caused me to get stung!" Caylem shouted, as he assessed his weals.

"Yeah, your chest is starting to blister...I feel sorry for him."

"You feel sorry for *him*?"

"If he was happy with himself he wouldn't enjoy hurting others so much."

"Well, he's really trying my patience."

"Forget him. I was about to go fishing, why don't you join me."

"Nah, I just got back from that."

"Come on, we can go past the shelf and see what's out there."

"No, it's not safe to go that far."

"Come on, don't be such a chicken."

"...What's a *'chicken'*?"

"Come on! Expand your horizons! There're probably all sorts of delicious fish out there waiting to be caught but you'll never know because the thought of leaving your comfort zone scares you so much. Besides, if you don't have any luck, I promise to catch something nice for you before we return."

"Alright, but let's not stay too long - okay?"

"Deal."

And with that, they sallied out to sea, striding the billows until the island was little more than a speck on the skyline behind them.

SHELF short for "insular shelf" [where the water suddenly gets much deeper]
STRIDING (STRIY-ding) swimming with long strokes
TENTACLES (TEHN-tuh-kuhls) long, flexible, boneless limbs
THRONG (THRAHNG) crowded group
UNFETTER (uhn-FEH-ter) free from restraint; release
WEALS (WEE-uhlz) swollen, red marks from being stung
YOWLED (YOWLD) cried out in pain

"This ought to be far enough," said Thera, after slowing her strokes. "Let's see what's down there!"

She drew a breath and dipped below the surface as Caylem prepared to follow - the notion of noshing on fish was appealing but did little to comfort his fluttery stomach.

With inflated lungs and renewed resolve, he discounted his disquiet and dove after her. The limpid water displayed

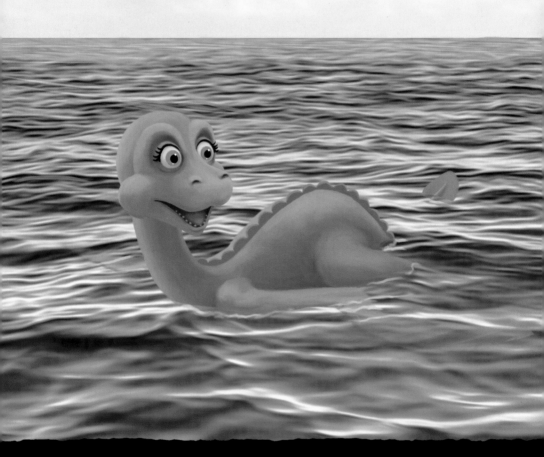

BATHYAL (BAA-thee-uhl) an oceanic zone with water too deep for sunlight to reach
DESCRIED (dehs-KRIYD) noticed, but with difficulty
DISCOUNTED (dihs-KOWN-tehd) deemed unimportant; ignored
DISQUIET (dihs-KWIY-eht) uneasy feeling
EAR SQUEEZE ear pain from increasing water pressure
ENQUIRY (EHN-kwer-ee) investigation
IMBUED (ihm-BYOOD) filled completely

brilliant sunbeams, but an areal search turned up no sign of life, so Thera motioned for him to follow her deeper. As they descended, the darkening water and onset of ear squeeze threatened their jaunt, but a light descried near bathyal depths impelled further enquiry; though paltry in size, it radiated with a seductive glow that imbued its vicinity.

By the time they reached the cusp of its flux a fish had appeared and was probing it, but what they now saw that the fish overlooked was the light had unfurled from the pate of a hideous anglerfish. The anglerfish furtively lowered its jaw while positioning itself to strike, then devoured its prey in a single gulp.

As they marveled at witnessing fate's ghastly praxis a second occurrence eclipsed what they spied; the angler itself became the collation of a massive megalodon that blitzed from below.

BLITZED (BLIHTST) suddenly attacked
COLLATION (koh-LAY-shuhn) light meal
CUSP (KUHSP) edge
ECLIPSED (eh-KLIHPST) overshadowed
FLUX (FLUHKS) flow
FURTIVELY (FER-tihv-lee) in a way to avoid being noticed
GHASTLY (GAAST-lee) frightful

HIDEOUS (HIH-dee-uhs) very ugly
MARVELED (MAHR-vehld) wondered
OCCURENCE (uh-KER-ehns) event
PATE (PAYT) top of the head
PRAXIS (PRAAK-sihs) way of happening
PROBING (PROH-bing) investigating
UNFURLED (uhn-FERLD) unrolled

COURSING (KAUR-sing) flowing without obstruction
HOMED (HOHMD) focused

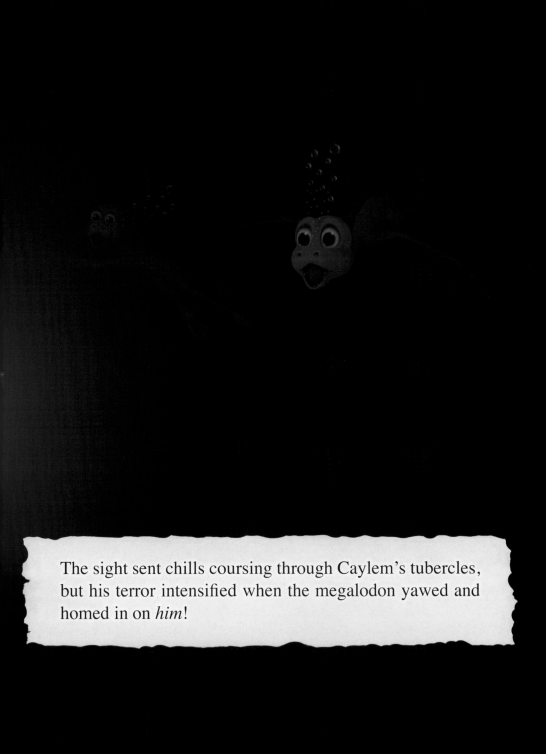

The sight sent chills coursing through Caylem's tubercles, but his terror intensified when the megalodon yawed and homed in on *him*!

TUBERCLES (TOO-ber-kuhlz) warty skin outgrowths
YAWED (YAUD) changed direction

EPINEPHRAL (eh-pih-NEH-fruhl) of epinephrine [a temporary strength boosting hormone]
FERVOR (FER-vaur) intense enthusiasm
JETTED (JEH-tehd) carried at jetlike speed

He pivoted upward and pumped his pectorals with an epinephral fervor that jetted him to the surface,

then burst from the water as the tine-lined chops of the megalodon gnashed behind him.

Now aloft, his vigorous flapping propelled him skyward, where oceanic zephyrs lent succor, along with the opportunity to reclaim lost composure.

The lofty perspective engendered an epiphany; his malformed flippers were fashioned for *flying*! - which begot him a rapturous glide back to shore. Upon reaching the sand, he canted his wings to stall his flight, but an ungainly touchdown sent him stumbling headlong into a stand of

ALOFT (uh-LAUFT) up in the air
CANTED (KAN-tehd) tilted
COMPOSURE (kuhm-POH-zher) state of calmness and self-control
ENGENDERED (ehn-JEHN-derd) caused to have
EPIPHANY (eh-PIH-feh-nee) a sudden and important realization
LOLLED (LAHLD) laid in a relaxed way
PHRAGMITES (fraag-MIY-teez) beach grass

phragmites, where a face-plant ended his escapade.

He raised his head to spit out a spikelet but remained prostrate to ponder the previous happening. How would he put his new talent to use? He lolled for a spell envisioning benefits, when a voice interrupted his reverie: "Hey look, it's 'Fail 'em Caylem'. He can't catch fish, so he has ta eat *grass* instead!"

PROSTRATE (PRAH-strayt) lying face down
RAPTUROUS (RAAP-cher-uhs) very pleasurable
REVERIE (REHV-eh-ree) daydreaming
SPIKELET (SPIYK-leht) small part of a grass flower
SUCCOR (SUH-kaur) aid in a time of difficulty
UNGAINLY (uhn-GAYN-lee) clumsy
ZEPHYRS (ZEH-ferz) gentle breezes

BOLSTERED (BOHL-sterd) propped up
CARRIAGE (KAA-raaj) body posture
DOMINATED (DAH-mih-nay-tehd) overpowered and controlled
GLARE (GLEAR) angry stare

Caylem looked back to find Olly with his friend and a couple of girls as the group broke into laughter.

"You haven't *failed* until you quit trying," he retorted, while rising to respond.

Olly stopped laughing and bolstered his carriage.

"You got somethin' ta say ta me puke?" he snapped with a glare.

Caylem stayed silent but stood his ground as the bully squared off and rushed him. He fought back with a vengeance and dominated the struggle, until Olly's friend joined in and the two overpowered him. After pinning him to the ground, they knelt on his wings to keep him down while Olly scooped a finful of sand.

RETORTED (reh-TAUR-tehd) cleverly replied
RUSHED (RUHSHT) charged at
SQUARED OFF took a fighting stance
VENGEANCE (VEHN-jehns) desire for revenge

"You better get use ta the taste of this," he taunted, between labored breaths. "…cuz it's all you'll ever be able ta catch!"

No sooner had Olly completed his utterance than the ground began to quake. A thunderous blast soon followed, causing all and sundry to recoil. The girls screamed as a muddle of molten rock and ash started spewing from the volcano at the center of the island.

RECOIL (REE-koy-ihl) pull back in horror
TAUNTED (TAUN-tehd) provoked anger by insulting

EJECTA (eh-JEHK-tuh) mixture of materials ejected from a volcano during eruption
FACULTY (FAA-kuhl-tee) power
HARROWING (HAA-roh-ing) terrifying
NEWFOUND (NOO-fownd) recently discovered

The harrowing sight sent everyone hurrying for the water but Caylem took to the air instead, where his newfound faculty transported him high above the ejecta. He soared with sangfroid in the serenity of the airspace while the turmoil transpired below.

SANGFROID (sahng-FWAH) calmness in a time of trouble
SERENITY (seh-REH-nih-tee) peacefulness
TRANSPIRED (trans-PIY-erd) happened
TURMOIL (TER-moy-uhl) trouble

By sunset, the seisms had ceased
and the tephra cloud tapered
but the prolonged solitude sparked introspection,
so he alit at the lagoon for further reflection.
After bedding down at the base of a boulder,
he reposed in the quiet with his sense of self in question.
Had conformity compromised nature's intention?
What one does best should dictate direction,
but he'd just been following other's suggestion
and now his condition required correction
before it resulted in utter abjection!

Maybe a fish could be caught from the air?
Stalked from above as it swam unaware.
How he would nab the thing still was unclear,
but the idea seemed worthy of testing with care.
Then again, what if it didn't work out?
Others might laugh at him, shame him with doubt,
voice disapproval and look down their snout,
making him wish he'd not taken that route.
Still, he'd be favoring faith over fear;
muster his courage and take on the dare.
In spite of how foolish it might appear,
the time to try fishing by flying was here.

ABJECTION (aab-JEHK-shuhn) misery from failure
ACQUIRED (uh-KWIY-erd) received
ALIT (uh-LIHT) landed
ASPIRED (uhs-PIY-erd) hoped for
AUDIBLE (AU-dih-buhl) able to be heard
CEASED (SEEST) stopped
COMPROMISED (KAHM-proh-miyzd) sacrificed
CONFORMITY (kuhn-FAWR-mih-tee) following what others approve of
DICTATE (DIHK-tayt) determine
FAITH (FAYTH) belief [in the absence of evidence]
INQUIRED (ihn-KWIY-erd) asked
INTENTION (ihn-TEHN-shuhn) plan
INTROSPECTION (ihn-troh-SPEHK-shuhn) self-examination
MIRED (MIY-erd) slowed progress

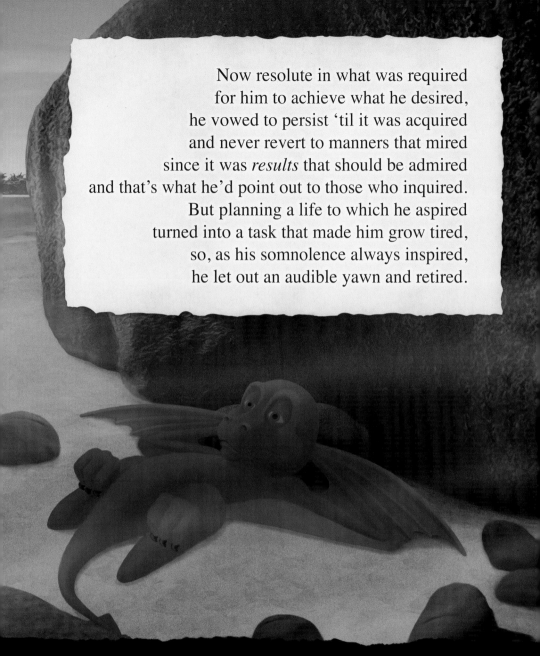

Now resolute in what was required
for him to achieve what he desired,
he vowed to persist 'til it was acquired
and never revert to manners that mired
since it was *results* that should be admired
and that's what he'd point out to those who inquired.
But planning a life to which he aspired
turned into a task that made him grow tired,
so, as his somnolence always inspired,
he let out an audible yawn and retired.

MUSTER (MUHS-ter) gather
PERSIST (per-SIHST) continue trying
PROLONGED (proh-LAUNGD) for an extended length of time
REFLECTION (reh-FLEHK-shuhn) review of past experiences
REPOSED (reh-POHZD) laid in a relaxed position
RESOLUTE (reh-zuh-LOOT) firm in belief and desire
RETIRED (reh-TIY-erd) went to sleep
SEISMS (SIY-zuhmz) earth shaking
SENSE OF SELF belief about who he was
SOLITUDE (SAH-lih-tood) time spent alone
SOMNOLENCE (SAHM-nuh-lehns) sleepiness
TAPERED (TAY-perd) reduced in size
TEPHRA (TEH-fruh) volcanic rock fragments
VOWED (VOWD) promised

CROUCH (KROWCH) low stance
ENTHRALLED (ehn-THRAULD) fascinated
ENTREATY (ehn-TREE-tee) urgent request; plea
ENVISAGED (ehn-VIH-sihjd) imagined [something not yet experienced]

7

Rise and Shine!

The next morning Caylem awoke to an importunate gastric entreaty and set out for something to satisfy it. While searching for lithodon under rocks near the edge of the water a flash of movement in the sky caught his eye. He lifted his head for a better look and dropped his jaw in amazement at the sight of a creature – similar to himself – flying toward the beach with a fish clutched in her talons. As he watched, she canted her wings and landed behind some boulders at the opposite end of the lagoon.

When she disappeared from view Caylem rose from his crouch and headed after her with a brisk gait. Were others already fishing as he envisaged? The prospect enthralled him, and he ached to find out.

GAIT (GAYT) pace of walking
GASTRIC (GAAS-trihk) of the stomach
IMPORTUNATE (ihm-PAUR-choo-neht) annoyingly persistent
PROSPECT (PRAH-spehkt) possibility of happening

COUNTERED (KOWN-terd) asserted in response
GRIPED (GRIYPT) complained

As he marched up to the boulders a pair of voices squabbled on the other side: "...and we should be out looking for her but now we're going to be stuck here for a while," the female griped.

"Well it's not my fault the volcano erupted!" the male rejoined.

"We wouldn't be in this situation if you'd been more considerate to begin with," she countered.

Caylem rounded the boulders to find a second creature gobbling down the fish the female had caught. He was seated on a rock with his wing held out as though it had been injured. The female sat nearby with a disgruntled deportment and looked up in surprise as he walked toward them.

"Excuse me," said Caylem. "I didn't mean to startle you. I saw you flying with a fish and was just wondering how you caught it."

"Well…" the male greeted with a smile, as he looked Caylem over. "We never expected to run into another uranosaur this far from the colony. What brought *you* out here?"

'Uranosaur?' Caylem pondered the term before answering. "…Oh, I'm with the *thallasaurs* - on the east shore," he replied. "I come here for lithodon on occasion - the rocks by the water are full of them."

"Ah, lithodon. I haven't had those in a while. They're all fished out where we live. I'll have to go for some later."

"Yeah, it's the same where I'm from but it's pretty secluded here. I'm 'Caylem', by the way."

"Nice to meet you Caylem. I'm 'Adelpho' and this is my mate, 'Lyzandra'. I'd shake your wing but mine's out of commission right now. We'll be camping here until it heals."

"What happened?"

PONDERED (PAHN-derd) thought carefully about
ROUNDED (ROWN-dehd) walked around
SECLUDED (seh-KLOO-dehd) not visited often
STARTLE (STAR-tuhl) take b ... prise

"*Karma*," Lyzandra facetiously interjected.

"Oh, stop," said Adelpho. "I was tagged by a rock from the volcano yesterday while we were out flying over the jungle."

"Oh no, are you okay?" asked Caylem.

"Yeah, it's just a sprain. Heh-heh, in a matter of seconds the sky transformed from a trove of tranquility to a gauntlet of gas and blazing boulders! Then the impact from the rock sent me tumbling through the treetops. I was lashed by leaves and battered by branches until I finally fell into one of those messy melabac bushes - you know, the ones with the bitter berries…"

"Yeah."

"…that's how I got all these sticky stains on myself."

"Well, I suppose that was better than falling into a *polentro* plant."

"Ha-ha! Yeah - with all those prickly protrusions - that would've finished me off for sure!"

"So, how did you end up *here*?"

"Well, I needed someplace to recover - but it wasn't going be in *there* - so we started walking."

"We couldn't get out of there fast enough," added

FACETIOUSLY (fuh-SEE-shuhs-lee) jokingly [in a sarcastic way]
GAUNTLET (GAUNT-leht) an attack from multiple sides at once
INTERJECTED (ihn-ter-JEHK-tehd) interrupted to insert
KARMA (KAHR-muh) living, what a person doing

Lyzandra.

"I was all scratched up and my elbow was hurting but I was more concerned with what we might run into than the shape I was in," Adelpho continued. "It took us a while to find our way out too."

"It was dark by the time we got here last night - and we were tired - so we skipped dinner and went to sleep, that's why I had to get some fishing done this morning," said Lyzandra. "…Speaking of which, I need to go for myself now. If you want to join me I can show you how I do it."

"That would be wonderful!" Caylem beamed.

Lyzandra stood from her rock and motioned for Caylem to follow her. "So, how are you fishing now?" she asked, as they walked toward the water together.

"I haven't actually caught anything yet," Caylem replied. "I'm still not fast enough, so my family's been helping me."

"I can relate. When I first started I struggled with my focus. I'd swoop down over a school of fish without singling one out and staying with it long enough to catch it. When you chase more than one, you end up with none."

EGRESSED (ee-GREHST) left
IN CONCERT together
LILT (LIHLT) manner of moving

When they came to the water they pushed off in concert and flew toward the reef with a synchronous lilt, then egressed the lagoon to seek their repasts in the resplendent waters of the open ocean.

"Over here!" called Lyzandra, after a period of winging. "I see breakfast…"

REPASTS (reh-PAASTS) meals
RESPLENDENT (rehs-PLEHN-dehnt) impressive in appearance
SYNCHRONOUS (SIN-kroh-nuhs) at the same time

Caylem looked on as she veered away and retracted her wings, then dropped to the water with extended talons and summarily plucked a sizable fish from the whitecaps.

"…How was that?" she smiled, upon returning with her catch.

"Awesome!" Caylem resounded.

"Give it a try. There's a whole school down there waiting for you."

EXTENDED (ehks-TEHN-dehd) held outward
RESOUNDED (reh-ZOWN-dehd) praised loudly
RETRACTED (reh-TRAAK-tehd) drew i

SUMMARILY (suh-MAA-rih-lee) casually
VEERED (VEARD) suddenly changed direction
WHITECAPS (WIYT-kaaps) foam crested waves

ACCEDED (aak-SEE-dehd) agreed [to follow a request]
APLOMB (uh-PLAHM) self-confidence [in a demanding situation]
BESTRIDING (beh-STRIY-ding) positioned with one leg on each side of
COUNSEL (KOWN-sehl) advice
DEPLOYED (deh-PLOYD) made use of
FORAY (fau-RAY) sudden attack
HEWED (HYOOD) followed as directed

Caylem replied with a fabulous foray - surgically striking the school with aplomb - but his sprightly quarry dodged his grasp and he returned to Lyzandra empty-handed.

"You've got to *lead* the fish," she said. "Touch down where you *expect* it to be and let it swim to you."

Caylem acceded and deployed his talons for an incursion that hewed to her counsel, then volplaned toward the water while targeting another catch...

Now bestriding a billow with self-belief strong,
he plunged both his raptor traps inside on song,
and, without fear of failure or doing it wrong,

INCURSION (ihn-KER-zhuhn) sudden invasion
ON SONG done very well
QUARRY (KWAU-ree) prey
RAPTOR TRAPS feet with talon tipped toes
SELF-BELIEF confidence in one's own ability
SPRIGHTLY (SPRIYT-lee) energetic
VOLPLANED (VAHL-playnd) dived in a controlled manner

...successfully seized what he'd sought for so long!

"Way to go, Caylem!" Lyzandra praised, as he circled back to her with his catch. "We've got to show Adelpho."

ACCLAIM (uh-KLAYM) enthusiastic praise
BASKED (BAASKT) took pleasure in
COUP (KOO) noteworthy success
DONNING (DAU-ning) wearing
INDOMITABLE (ihn-DAH-mih-tuh-buhl) unbeatable

Caylem basked in her acclaim donning an indomitable visage and vaunted his coup with a triumphant tenor while navigating gusts back to the lagoon.

NAVIGATING (NAA-vih-gay-ting) maneuvering through
TENOR (TEH-ner) high-pitched voice
TRIUMPHANT (triy-UHM-fant) victorious
VAUNTED (VAUN-tehd) enthusiastically boasted
VISAGE (VIH-zihj) facial expression

When they got back to the boulders he held up his trophy for an impromptu inspection as Adelpho and Lyzandra looked on.

"That's a fine-looking fish," Adelpho commended.

"That's his first catch," Lyzandra apprised.

"Really? Congratulations Caylem! You never forget your first catch."

"Thanks," Caylem grinned, before scarfing it down.

"Yeah, I remember mine…" Adelpho continued. "I was with my father when I caught it. He'd spent most of the day showing me how, but I wasn't having any luck. Then, just as the sun was setting, I finally snagged one."

"You must have been excited."

"*Oh* yeah. I couldn't wait to show my mother, so I raced back to the nest with it. She was brooding an egg there at the time - and always kept it protected - but when she got up to congratulate me a lestedrom came and stole it."

"Oh, wow."

"Yeah, she went berserk and chased it into the jungle - but after that we never saw her again."

"Oh, sorry to hear that."

"…I guess you have to expect the unexpected."

"For sure."

"…So, how long have you been with the thallasaurs?"

"All my life."

APPRISED (uh-PRIYZD) informed
BERSERK (ber-ZERK) crazy
BROODING (BROO-ding) sitting on to hatch
COMMENDED (kuh-MEHN-dehd) praised

"Hmm. ...I've seen them in the *water*. You're a *sky* lizard Caylem."

Just then the crackle of footsteps tolled from a nearby thicket.

"Shh, something's coming!" Lyzandra warned.

IMPROMPTU (ihm-PRAHMP-too) unplanned
SCARFING (SKAHR-fing) eating very quickly
THICKET (THIH-keht) dense group of bushes
TOLLED (TOHLD) sounded

113

AFORE (uh-FAUR) before
COLLOQUY (KAH-luh-kwee) conversation
COMELY (KUHM-lee) good looking

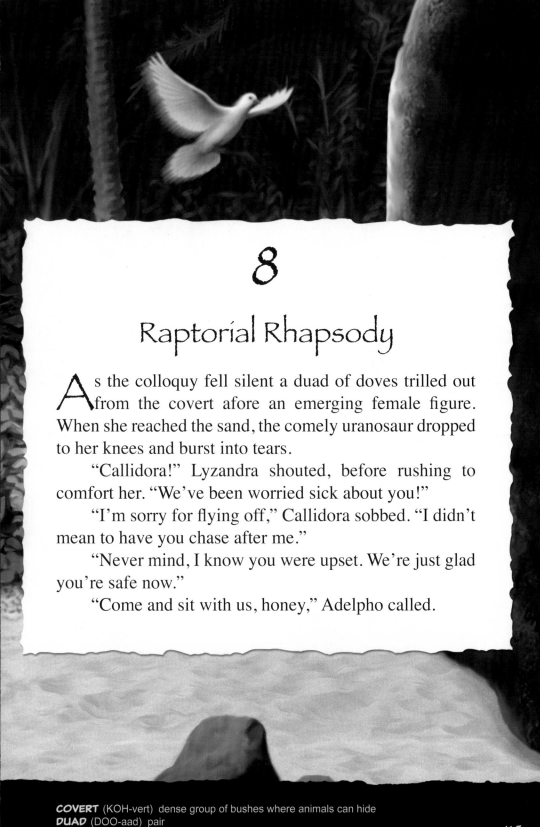

8

Raptorial Rhapsody

As the colloquy fell silent a duad of doves trilled out from the covert afore an emerging female figure. When she reached the sand, the comely uranosaur dropped to her knees and burst into tears.

"Callidora!" Lyzandra shouted, before rushing to comfort her. "We've been worried sick about you!"

"I'm sorry for flying off," Callidora sobbed. "I didn't mean to have you chase after me."

"Never mind, I know you were upset. We're just glad you're safe now."

"Come and sit with us, honey," Adelpho called.

COVERT (KOH-vert) dense group of bushes where animals can hide
DUAD (DOO-aad) pair
TRILLED (TRIHLD) chirped with a quiver

"What's wrong with your wing?" Callidora asked, as Lyzandra escorted her over.

"I hurt it yesterday but it's already feeling much better. Have you been in the jungle all this time?"

"When the volcano went off I went there to hide, but

ALACRITOUS (uh-LAA-krih-tuhs) very enthusiastic
COZY (KOH-zee) comfortable and relaxed
ESCORTED (ehs-KAUR-tehd) walked with

after spending the night I couldn't find my way out until I heard your voices and followed them."

"Well, I'm sorry for losing my temper with you yesterday. I shouldn't have yelled the way I did."

"No, I'm sorry for complaining about the fish you catch. I really do appreciate all you and Lyzandra do for me."

"Callidora, this is 'Caylem'," said Lyzandra, with a genial gesture in his direction. "We met him here earlier. He just caught his first fish a little while ago. And Caylem, this is my sister, 'Callidora'. She's still learning to fish, so we've been helping her."

After exchanging greetings with Callidora, Caylem was rapt, and the subsequent hours he spent chatting with her and the others seemed to pass like minutes for him. When the conversation finally waned, the sun had sunk substantially and Callidora was getting hungry.

"I haven't eaten all day," she said. "Would someone mind catching something for me?"

"It's kind of late to fish now," Lyzandra replied, from a cozy cuddle with Adelpho. "Why don't you go with Caylem for some lithodon?"

"That sounds good," said Callidora. "Are there any around here?"

"Yeah," said Caylem, with an alacritous intonation. "Come on, I'll show you."

INTONATION (ihn-toh-NAY-shuhn) sound of voice
RAPT (RAAPT) totally fascinated by
SUBSTANTIALLY (suhb-STAN-chuh-lee) to a great extent

Callidora perked up and went with him to the foreshore where they spent time enjoying the littoral creatures. While upending rocks in the lambent sunlight she stopped to admire the splendorous environs, but the ambience changed when she stepped near the water and something took hold of her ankle.

AMBIENCE (AM-bee-ehns) character and mood of a place
ENVIRONS (ehn-VIY-ruhns) surroundings
FORESHORE (FAUR-shaur) land near the water at low tide
LAMBENT (LAM-behnt) softly lighted

LITTORAL (LIH-tau-ruhl) of the shore
SPLENDOROUS (SPLEHN-dau-ruhs) absolutely beautiful
UPENDING (uh-PEHN-ding) turning over

She looked down in horror to find a terrifying titanoboa tenaciously tugging her toward the flood tide. As the whelming water mantled her plight she fought to break free with a frenzy of flailing and frenetic wing flapping, but her efforts proved futile against the sinewy serpent's superior strength.

FLAILING (FLAY-ih-ling) wild swinging
FRENETIC (freh-NEH-tihk) energetic and uncontrolled
FUTILE (FYOO-tihl) useless
INVIOLABLE (ihn-VIY-uh-luh-buhl) unbreakable
LEVIATHAN (leh-VIY-uh-thuhn) very large creature of the water
MANTLED (MAN-tuhld) covered

When Caylem heard her blood-curdling cries he cut short his rootling and rushed to her rescue. After entering the water, he stooped down and snapped at the snake's scaly snoot - hoping to halt it from harming his heroine - but the voracious leviathan's vim was inviolable.

ROOTLING (ROO-tuh-ling) searching through casually
SINEWY (SIHN-yoo-ee) muscular
SNOOT (SNOOT) nose
TENACIOUSLY (teh-NAY-shuhs-lee) with determination
VIM (VIHM) will
VORACIOUS (vau-RAY-shuhs) very hungry
WHELMING (WEHL-ming) engulfing

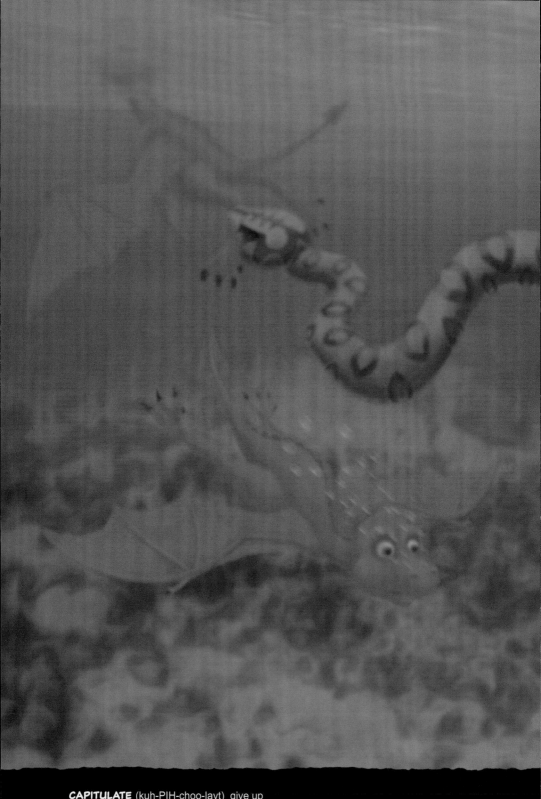

CAPITULATE (kuh-PIH-choo-layt) give up
CONCEDED (kuhn-SEE-dehd) accepted to be true
DEMISE (deh-MIYZ) death
DREADFUL (DREHD-fuul) with great suffering

With water now nearing the nape of her neck, Callidora conceded her dreadful demise but Caylem refused to capitulate. In a last-ditch endeavor to foil her foe, he dove underwater, took hold of its tail, and, just as it seemed Callidora was doomed,

ENDEAVOR (ehn-DEH-vaur) attempt [at something important]
FOE (FOH) enemy
FOIL (FOY-uhl) stop from succeeding
NAPE (NAYP) back of the neck

surged through the surface with it clasped in his talons! As he raised the reptile over the water it released Callidora and refocused on him.

CLASPED (KLAASPT) held tightly

While warding off wounds from unsettling strikes he soared with the saurian to the vent of the volcano, where he verbalized ire and dropped it inside.

VENT (VEHNT) opening
VERBALIZED (VER-buh-liyzd) put into words
WARDING (WAUR-ding) guarding against

When he returned to the lagoon, Callidora sat shoreside sniffling softly in solace.

"Hold me," she murmured with lachrymose eyes, as he walked up to comfort her.

"Are you okay?" Caylem asked, with an enfolding wing.

"…When I was ready to learn how to fish my father took me out over the ocean to watch how he did it. As we were flying, he spotted a school and went down to catch one but when he got to the water a plesiosaur swam up and grabbed him. All I could do was scream as it pulled him under, and ever since then, I haven't been able to fly near the water without panicking."

"I'm sorry about your father, Callidora - that was a terrible thing for you to witness. The water *does* have ugliness, but you need to know that it also has a lot of beauty."

ENFOLDING (ehn-FOHL-ding) hugging
LACHRYMOSE (LAAK-rih-mohs) tearful

PLESIOSAUR (PLEE-see-uh-saur) large, prehistoric ocean creature
SOLACE (SAH-laas) comfort in a time of sorrow

ATTESTATION (aa-teh-STAY-shuhn) proof of claims made
DULCET (DUHL-seht) soothing
ENTHRALLMENT (ehn-THRAUL-mehnt) deep fascination
EXHORTED (ehks-HAUR-tehd) urged strongly
FLUORESCED (flau-REHST) glowed brightly
HIED (HIYD) went quickly

Later that evening they nestled in the moonlight to a dulcet cantabell tintinnabulation. As Caylem related grand submarine sightings he paused in remembrance of one she might like.

"Wait here!" he exhorted on impulse, while standing. "I'll be right back!"

As Callidora awaited he launched himself skyward and hied to the ocean, then dove to the floor for a clam's attestation. Upon his return he proffered a pearl of astonishing size that fluoresced with a mesmeric shimmer.

"This is for you," he smiled.

"Ah, Caylem!" gasped Callidora, as she accepted it from him. "It's incredible!"

After a prolonged period of wide-eyed enthrallment, Callidora looked up and expressed more delight: "The colors are just amazing! Isn't this the most beautiful thing you've ever seen?"

MESMERIC (mehz-MEH-rihk) hypnotic
NESTLED (NEH-suhld) snuggled
RELATED (ree-LAY-tehd) told of
REMEMBRANCE (reh-MEHM-brehns) the act of remembering
SUBMARINE (SUHB-muh-reen) underwater
TINTINNABULATION (tihn-tihn-aab-yoo-LAY-shuhn) tinkling sound

ELECTRIFYING (eh-LEHK-trih-fiy-ing) thrilling
EMBRACE (ehm-BRAYS) tight hold
OSCULATION (ahs-kyoo-LAY-shuhn) kiss

"…Almost," replied Caylem, with a heartfelt embrace.

Callidora got quiet as his snout drew near and puckered her lips to requite his affection. Now gripped by desire, and postured to slake, they lost themselves in an electrifying osculation.

POSTURED (PAHS-cherd) positioned [as in pose of the body]
REQUITE (reh-KWIYT) return what is offered; reciprocate
SLAKE (SLAYK) satisfy

AFFIRMED (uh-FERMD) maintained as true
AIR (EAR) manner of behavior
BESTOWAL (beh-STOH-uhl) gift
ENSORCELLMENT (ehn-SAUR-sehl-mehnt) as if under a magic spell
JESTED (JEHS-tehd) joked

9

Provenance qua Providence

The following morning the twosome returned to their siblings' locale sporting self-possessed smiles and an air of ensorcellment.

"What a lovely stone," Lyzandra remarked, on her sister's bestowal. "Where did you find it?"

"It's a *pearl*," beamed Callidora. "Caylem got it for me from the ocean."

"Gee, *I've* never gotten a gift like that from the ocean," Lyzandra jested, with a glance toward Adelpho.

"Well, I'm not much of a swimmer," Adelpho retorted, while flexing his wing. "...but I am feeling ready to fly again."

"Do you think you can make it back home today?"

"Yeah, let's leave after breakfast. ...Are you coming with us Caylem?"

"I am," affirmed Caylem. "...but I need to say 'bye' to my sister first. Eat without me and I'll meet you here later."

LOCALE (loh-KAAL) location
RETORTED (reh-TAUR-tehd) replied cleverly
SELF-POSSESSED calm and confident
SPORTING (SPAUR-ting) wearing
TWOSOME (TOO-suhm) couple

On his flight to find Thera, Caylem conjectured she'd show alongshore and restricted his search to the strand. As he soared in accord toward the thallasaur horde a rumpus erupted beneath him.

"Hey! Give it back!" a young thallasaur demanded, as Olly made off with his catch.

Olly obliged by offering it back, but just as the juvenile reached to retrieve it he flipped the fish to his friend with a titter to kick off a contest of 'keep away'.

ACCORD (uh-KAURD) harmony
CONJECTURED (kuhn-JEHK-cherd) figured
ERUPTED (eh-RUHP-tehd) became active
HORDE (HAURD) large group

OBLIGED (uh-BLIYJD) cooperated
RESTRICTED (reh-STRIHK-tehd) limited
RUMPUS (RUHM-puhs) noisy disturbance
TITTER (TIH-ter) giggle

137

As the bullies delighted in teasing their target Caylem swooped down and disrupted the disport by snatching the fish when the friend flung it back.

"Looks like persistence pays off," he quipped, before returning the fish to its rightful recipient.

Olly stood stifled from stark stupefaction as Caylem flew off to resume finding Thera.

DELIGHTED (deh-LIY-tehd) took pleasure
DISPORT (dihs-PAURT) 'fun'
DISRUPTED (dihs-RUHP-tehd) interrupted
PERSISTENCE (per-SIHS-tehns) not giving up
138 **QUIPPED** (KWIHPD) cleverly remarked

ADVERSITY (aad-VER-sih-tee) serious difficulty
ALIT (uh-LIHT) landed
ASTONISHMENT (uh-STAH-nihsh-mehnt) great surprise
CONFIRMED (kuhn-FERMD) assured

When he spotted her sunning herself on the sand, Caylem swept down and alit alongside her, stirring astonishment with his arrival.

"Caylem!" she shouted, with sheer incredulity. "You can *fly!*"

"And *fish*, forbye," he added with a smile.

"I feared the megalodon had gotten you."

"Adversity brought out the best in me instead."

"Well thank goodness I haven't seen the last of you," she sighed with a hug.

"Not yet," confirmed Caylem, "…but I've met someone special and I'm moving to the other side of the island to be with her."

"Oh Caylem, I'm happy for you! Promise you'll be back to visit."

"I will, and until then I'll miss you."

FORBYE (faur-BIY) as well
INCREDULITY (ihn-kreh-DOO-lih-tee) disbelief
SHEER (SHEAR) pure
STIRRING (STER-ring) causing strong emotion

After an affecting adieu, Caylem took wing and went back to the lagoon to accompany his compeers back home. With erstwhile sufferings fully surmounted, he appeared primed for a prosperous future.

Adelpho (uh-DEHL-foh) —

Bellusala (beh-luh-SAH-luh) —

Callidora (kaa-lih-DAU-ruh) —

Cantabell (KAN-tuh-behl) —

Caylem (KAY-luhm) —

Cryptognat (KRIHP-toh-naat) —

Dryptocaud (DRIHP-toh-kaud) —

Lestedrom (LEHS-teh-drahm) —

Lithodon (LIH-thoh-dahn) —

Lyzandra (lih-ZAHN-druh) —

Melabac (MEH-luh-bahk) —

Olly (AH-lee) —

Polentro (poh-LEHN-troh) —

Saltoneus (SAUL-tuh-noos) —

Thallasaur (THAAL-uh-saur) —

Thera (THEA-ruh) —

Uranosaur (er-RAN-oh-saur) —

Yarma (YAHR-muh) —

Zayle (ZAY-ihl) —